For Eunice - DM

GERDA THE GOOSE
Written by Hiawyn Oram
Illustrated by David Melling
British Library Cataloguing in Publication Data
A catalogue record of this book is available from the British Library
ISBN 0 340 74417 0 (HB)
ISBN 0 340 74418 9 (PB)
Text copyright © 2000 Hiawyn Oram
Illustrations copyright © 2000 David Melling

First edition published 2000
10 9 8 7 6 5 4 3 2 1

Published by Hodder Children's Books,
a division of Hodder Headline,
338 Euston Road, London NW1 3BH

Printed in Hong Kong

Gerda the Goose

Hiawyn Oram

Illustrated by
David Melling

h
Hodder
Children's
Books

A division of Hodder Headline

Gerda the Goose wanted to fly to the moon.
"Ridiculous," said the other geese.
"No one can get to the moon. You really are just
about the silliest silly goose any of us have ever
heard of."

But Gerda was
not giving up.
She packed a bag . . .

with two special
pebbles . . .

and her
lucky feather.

"It is only a matter of
a launching pad," she said,
"which right this minute,
I'm away to find."

And off she walked,
walked and waddled,
until she came to a lake.
On the edge of the lake was
an artist eagle with his easel
up and his paints spread around.
"Hello," said Gerda.
"Hello, Silly Goose," said the eagle.
"I am on my way to the moon," said Gerda,
"but as I am here I can't help noticing the
beautiful green of your lake."
"Ah yes," said the eagle. "I mix that green with
blue and yellow, a touch of purple and the tippiest
brush-tip of brown."

"Well I never! And who would have thought it?"
sighed Gerda. "Blue and yellow, a touch of purple
and the tippiest brush-tip of brown!"

And on she
walked,
walked and
waddled, until
she came to a quarry.

In the quarry were two miner
moles with their faces dirty and
their equipment lying around.
"Hello," said Gerda.
"Hello, Silly Goose," said the moles.

"I am on my way to the moon," said Gerda, "but as I was passing I couldn't help noticing you're not digging today."

"Not digging today, not digging no more," said the moles. "For we dug this mine the whole year long and not one lump of coal have we found."

"Well I never! And who would have thought it?" said Gerda picking out a small stone from the rubble and polishing it on her feathers. "That must be because this is a *diamond mine!*"

And on she walked, walked and waddled, until she came to a baker's shop.

In the shop was a baker mouse with his bread unbaked and his tarts unfilled but his singing voice ringing around.

"Hello," said Gerda.

"Hello, Silly Goose," said the mouse.

"I am on my way to the moon," said Gerda,

"but as I was passing I thought I heard the most beautiful song in the world."

"You did," said the Mouse. "It's *The Duckling's Song* from *The Flying Goose Opera* and I was singing it but you can get it from any old record shop just over the bridge in town."

"Well I never! And who would have thought it?" sighed Gerda. "A song like that, from any old record shop, just over the bridge in town!"

And on she walked, walked and waddled,
until she came to an observatory.
In the observatory was a moonologist owl
looking through a powerful telescope.
"Well, this is a bit of luck," said Gerda.
"What is?" said the moonologist.
"Meeting you," said Gerda, "because I'm
on my way to the moon and if you can't
point me in the right direction, who can?"

"Well . . ." said the owl, "as it happens, there's a launching pad right down the road. A rocket's just left but there'll be another one along in a minute. Meanwhile, if you're so interested why not take a look from here."

So Gerda put her eye to the owl's telescope and when she'd looked at the moon close up she put her head to one side and said, "Well I never! And who would have thought it? What a silly old goose I've been!"

And off she walked, walked and waddled
to sell her diamond and buy . . .

an old record-player,

The Flying Goose Opera,

some paints, brushes,

canvasses and
a folding easel . . .

. . . and walk and waddle
and waddle and walk all the way home.

"Hello!" she said when she arrived. "Hello!" cried the other geese, crowding round. "You've been gone so long, you must have been gone somewhere. Now hurry and tell us, what did you find?"

"I found anyone can go to the moon," said Gerda unpacking her paints, "from the launch pad over the hill. Though take it from me, that moon up there is cold and bleak and not at all the kind of place to be!"

B

ut the geese weren't listening.

They were packing and pushing . . .

. . . and rushing and racing.

They were off . . . to walk and waddle, waddle and walk to the launch pad over the hill.

And as Gerda set up her easel and wound up her record-player, she watched them go and sighed, "Well I never! And what a bit of luck . . .

a perfect day . . . the perfect place . . .

". . . and not a single silly goose around!"